The Fake Date

Ayshia Monroe

Bein' Good	Fitting In
Blind Trust	Holding Back
Diva	Keepin' Her Man
Doin' It	Stalked
The Fake Date	Tempted

www.sdlback.com

Copyright ©2012 by Saddleback Educational Publishing

All rights reserved. No part of this book may be reproduced in any form or by any means, electronic or mechanical, including photocopying, recording, scanning, or by any information storage and retrieval system, without the written permission of the publisher. SADDLEBACK EDUCATIONAL PUBLISHING and any associated logos are trademarks and/or registered trademarks of Saddleback Educational Publishing.

ISBN-13: 978-1-61651-667-3
ISBN-10: 1-61651-667-4
eBook: 978-1-61247-639-1

Printed in Guangzhou, China
0712/CA21201001

16 15 14 13 12   1 2 3 4 5

[CHAPTER]

1

"Prom? Whatchu sayin', Tia? You sayin' we all gotta show up at prom, Tee-YUH?"

Marnyke Cooper deliberately mispronounced the name of the South Central High School yearbook manager, Tia Ramirez. She knew Tia hated when Marnyke did that, which was exactly why Marnyke did it. Tia had been off Marnyke's top-ten classmates list since a few months before when she'd tried to break up Marnyke and Marnyke's boyfriend, the senior basketball star Darnell Watson.

Half the time, Marnyke forgave Tia. The other half of the time, she didn't.

Right now, she didn't.

"That's exactly what I'm saying, Mar-NEEK," Tia replied.

Marnyke rolled her well-made-up eyes at Tia's weak comeback. "Then you be trippin', Tee-YUH. Everybody knows prom be wack!"

It was late May, and one of the last yearbook club meetings of the school year. Marnyke wasn't a member of yearbook club—everybody called it YC—by choice. She'd been ordered there as punishment by Mr. Crandall, the mean guidance counselor. He said she'd cut too many classes and skipped too many days.

Most YC meetings, Marnyke tried to be the last one in Ms. Okoro's classroom. Today, though, she'd been the second to show. Tia was already there, of course. She was a go-getter to the max, which made her extremely annoying. Right away, Tia had tried to get Marnyke excited about the junior-senior prom that was coming up on Saturday night.

"Prom doesn't have to be—how did you put it, Marnyke? Oh yes. 'Wack,'" Tia responded. She still had a little bit of an accent from her native Mexico. A little taller than Marnyke, with thick dark hair and round glasses, Tia wore the kind of pantsuit that a girl might wear to a job interview. "Prom can actually be fun. Especially if everyone shows up and helps."

Marnyke shook her head disdainfully. "Maybe where you from, *chica*, prom be cool. But lemme break it down for you. Here it be in the lame cafeteria with el-lame-o decorations. That make it wack!"

More kids had filed into Ms. O's room for the YC meeting, and they all laughed.

There was Marnyke's bestie, jockish Kiki Butler, who wore her usual basketball kicks, battered jeans, and a T-shirt. There was Kiki's twin sister, Sherise, who was prettier than Kiki but who dressed like a goody-two-shoes white girl. Sherise sat with her boyfriend, handsome Carlos Howard. Like Darnell, Carlos had a gang background but was now out of the life. Just coming into the room was curvy Nishell Saunders in a brown dress and sandals. She was the main yearbook photographer, and, as usual, she had her camera around her neck. Right behind Nishell was class clown Jackson Beauford, and his newcomer friend, Lattrell Chance.

Darnell was missing this meeting. He'd been excused to take his mom to the doctor.

"That's fine," Marnyke thought. "Ain't nothing important gonna happen."

Ms. Okoro, the yearbook advisor and English teacher who everyone called Ms. O, stepped into the fray.

"Marnyke? Tia?" she cautioned in her soft Nigerian accent. "How do you kids say it? Take a cool pill and sit down."

"You mean 'chill pill,' Ms. O!" Jackson shouted.

Ms. O smiled. "Yes. Chill pill. I'm sorry. I still don't have all the American slang. Anyway, don't forget the good work we did this year."

The club had done some good things, for sure. The yearbook had been nominated for a big prize until Mr. Crandall had banned it after a hacked and Photoshopped picture of his bare behind had been inserted as the centerfold.

"It's just that Tia think she better than everyone," Marnyke mused as she took a seat in the second row. "Well, she ain't better 'n me at gettin' a man!"

When it came to guys, Marnyke had Tia dusted. She figured that was why Tia, who was on prom committee, wanted her so badly. If Marnyke said that prom was cool, a whole lot of people would suddenly want to attend.

Marnyke was a boy magnet. Petite, with long legs and serious twins, she was the flyest girl at South Central High School. Her waist was tiny, her hair lustrous, and her eyes changed color depending on her mood. She was also a genius at hair, makeup, and dressing on a budget. Today, for example, she wore a gray sleeveless shift dress with strappy sandals that showed off her toned calves. She'd found the dress for ten bucks at a used clothing shop in the Korean section of town.

For Marnyke, thrift shops were a must. She shared a one-bedroom apartment with her big sister, Akira. Their dad was long gone, and their mother was in prison on drug charges. Akira did okay, waitressing at a fancy downtown joint called Citron. But before her sister had found that job, they'd been regulars at the food bank.

Tia turned around to face the other kids. "Look, I know a lot of you think prom is stupid."

"Not stupid, Tia. Didn't you hear Marnyke? Prom be wack!" Jackson shouted.

"Wack," Tia corrected herself. "I know we can't afford a hotel. I know we can't afford a band. I know the decorations are homemade. But what about school spirit, you guys? Yearbook club has to be a leader. Right, Sherise?"

All eyes swung to Sherise Butler, the official yearbook president who'd been happy to let Tia do most of the work. Barely five feet tall, Sherise had shoulder-length dark hair, caramel-colored skin, and a very cute nose.

But she dress like a prissy white girl. Look at her, in them silk pants and frilly top. Little Miz Better Homes and Gardens*!*

Sherise seemed torn. "Well—"

"I got me an idea!" Jackson interrupted. "Let's do prom at the No-Tell Motel on Randolph Street. We can rent the whole place by the hour!"

The kids laughed. Even Ms. O cracked a smile. Just then, the classroom door opened. Marnyke expected to see mean Mr. Crandall storming in to yell at them. He hated when kids had fun, and he hated yearbook club.

Of course, that fake picture of his butt hadn't help.

It wasn't Crandall, though. Instead, their surprise visitor was a rangy African

American man in his fifties. He wore rumpled black pants, a shirt, and a tie.

Marnyke didn't recognize him. But Sherise apparently did.

"Big Boss!" Sherise jumped up, rushing to the door. "Everyone, this is 'Big Boss' Dawkins. His print shop did our yearbook. An' it wasn't his fault it got hacked, neither."

Marnyke had never met Big Boss, but like everyone in the city, she knew of him. He'd gone to South Central High School many years ago, and then played Major League Baseball. He'd even pitched for the Dodgers. After he retired, he came back to the hood to open his print shop. It was his shop that had printed the yearbook with the hacked picture of Mr. Crandall's naked rear end.

"Hey, Sherise," Big Boss said. "Sorry to walk in like this, Ms. Okoro."

The teacher from Nigeria gave a little wave. "What brings you back to high school, Big Boss? Feeling nostalgic for *Silas Marner*? Or maybe *The Red Badge of Courage*?"

"Never read 'em, sorry," Big Boss confessed. "But I do have something to say to your students."

"Then you've come to the right place. Tia and Sherise, please give our guest the floor."

Marnyke watched as Big Boss loped to the front of the room. He still moved like an athlete.

"Okay, here's why I'm here," Big Boss's voice rumbled. "I feel like I owe you kids somethin' after what happened with your yearbook."

"It wasn't your fault," Tia reminded him.

"How 'bout a thousand dollars apiece?" Jackson suggested.

The kids laughed. Jackson thought he was all that. He wasn't, but he was almost always funny.

Big Boss pointed at Jackson. "That's a thought, but I'm thinkin' something better. Not just for you, but for the whole school. I hear you have a prom comin' up."

Tia raised her hand. Big Boss nodded at her.

"We do. But no one wants to come," Tia said.

"You blame them?" Big Boss shook his head. "Your prom's in the same place it was when I went to this school. The cafeteria. Who wants a big party the same place you eat free breakfast? You kids deserve a prom someplace fresh."

"Where you got in mind?" Jackson asked. "The White House?"

People laughed again.

Big Boss waited for the room to quiet and then continued, "How about the

Excelsior Ballroom at the Hotel San Marino? With everything on me? An' I mean everything. It's my fault your yearbook got banned. I really want to make it up to you."

The kids sat in stunned silence. The San Marino was the nicest hotel in the city. It had a thousand rooms, ballrooms, restaurants, pools, a spa, gym, and whatnot. Marnyke had never been inside but had walked past it. The circular driveway was always filled with horse-drawn carriages, limousines, and expensive cars.

Tia was the first to react.

"Are you serious?" she asked Big Boss. "That'll cost a fortune!"

Big Boss nodded. "I socked away a lot of money from the majors. An' my business had a great year. I can afford it."

"What about Crandall?" Sherise queried.

"I asked. It's fine with him," Big Boss declared. "As long as no school money is involved."

The classroom erupted in cheers, whooping, and hollering. Prom at the San Marino? This was like a dream come true.

"I'd say thanks are in order," Ms. O said when things had calmed down a bit.

A moment later Big Boss was surrounded by students. The girls were hugging him; the guys were fist-bumping. Marnyke found herself right in the middle of the celebration with one fun question on her mind.

How Darnell gonna ask me to be his date?

CHAPTER 2

"Welcome to Citron." The hostess was a beautiful white girl with silky blond hair. She wore a short black dress and heels with a citron-colored scarf. "You're Marnyke Cooper?"

Marnyke looked around a little uncertainly. Citron was one of the best restaurants in the city. Also one of the priciest. Akira had been working there for about three months. It was hard to believe that she was about to meet Darnell here. When they went out, they usually ended up at Mio's pizza joint.

"That's me," Marnyke nodded. She felt her phone vibrate in her handbag and took it out. All afternoon it had been buzzing with texts about who had invited whom to prom. "Excuse me," she told the hostess.

"No worries," the hostess said. "You're our guest."

This text was from Kiki.

> Yes! Sean asked me!

Good fo' her. Sean King's the only dude she's ever liked.

Now, it's my turn.

The hostess smiled when Marnyke put her phone away. "Your sister, Akira, is my favorite waitress. Follow me. I just seated your date."

It was only few hours after Big Boss had made the announcement about prom. Somehow, on crazy short notice, Darnell had set up this romantic dinner for two. Once upon a time, Citron had been an egg warehouse. All the cooling pipes were still visible, but a million-dollar project had redone the place in pastel shades of yellow. The owners had hired the head chef away from Donald Trump. It was impossible to get a table. Darnell had somehow gotten one.

How he gonna pay for this?

Across the floor, Marnyke saw her sister taking an order. She looked beautiful in the gray skirt and citron-colored blouse that all the female servers wore. Akira looked up, saw Marnyke, and gave a little wave.

Marnyke got plenty of attention as she crossed the main floor of the restaurant. She'd changed into a short white linen dress with a wide black belt and black fishnet stockings. Then she spotted Darnell at a quiet table for two. He wore a fancy dark suit, white shirt, and red tie. With a high forehead, close-cropped hair, and a soul patch on his chin, Marnyke thought he was the handsomest guy she'd ever met. He played point guard, and he was headed for Long Beach State on a hoops scholarship after graduation.

"He come a long way," Marnyke thought as Darnell embraced her. At six foot three, he towered over her. *No one would guess my man got a past he ain't proud of.*

"Darnell, I don't know how you did this, but I love it," Marnyke said when she was settled in.

Darnell looked sheepish. "I called your sister. She got me the table and her employee discount too."

"That's called takin' advantage of the situation," Marnyke told him as a Latino busboy poured ice water into long-stem glasses. "You got mad skills."

Darnell smiled. "You look great, Marnyke."

"Thanks. You up on prom four-one-one? Jackson's goin' with Nishell. Carlos asked Sherise. I hear Tia's goin' with that guy Ty. Even Kiki got a date—Sean be goin' with her."

Darnell whistled. "I can't believe what Big Boss be doin' for us."

Darnell took a sip of water, and Marnyke felt sure that he was about to ask her to prom right now. She was ready to say yes. She could picture their big entrance. Everyone would see that even after this crazy year, she had the finest man in the school.

Maybe we gonna be voted prom king and queen. It could happen.

"Mar ... mar ... nyke," Darnell's voice cracked nervously. "I wonder if—"

"Good evening. I'm Mario, and I'll be your waiter for the evening."

An elegant man with an Italian accent had approached with two leather-bound menus. He wore a gray suit and a citron-colored tie. "We're glad to have you at Citron. The specials are on the handwritten sheet inside the menu. I recommend the monkfish or the short ribs in port-wine glaze. I'll be back soon if you have any questions."

Mario handed them the menus then moved away.

Darnell opened his; Marnyke figured they would order before he popped the question. She wanted something that wouldn't splatter on her dress, so she chose the lobster ravioli in fresh cream sauce with a hand-picked Sungold tomato salad. Darnell said he'd have the strip steak and sweet potato fries. She asked him whether he wanted to try the monkfish. He said he didn't eat nothing named after no jungle creatures.

When Mario returned, Darnell ordered for them both. Marnyke felt taken care of. This was a rare feeling. With no father and her mother in jail, most of the time she had to fend for herself.

"Don't worry none 'bout the check," Darnell told Marnyke when Mario had moved off. "I've got it worked out with your sister."

Marnyke fluttered her eyelashes. "Sounds like you got everything worked out. Hope maybe you gonna work me out after prom."

Okay. That was a bald-ass flirt.

Again, Darnell got that nervous look in his eyes.

"Now," Marnyke thought. "He gonna ask me now. Can I answer by kissin' him?"

"Marnyke, you a great girl," Darnell told her.

"You think?" She batted her naturally long eyelashes.

"You slammin'. You got the face, you got the body, you got the heart, an' you got the soul. You gonna go far."

"The only place I want to go is to prom with you, Darnell." Under the table, she brushed one of her feet against Darnell's shins, hoping he'd feel it.

"I don't know how to ask this, Marnyke," Darnell continued.

"Jus' ask," Marnyke encouraged. It was so sweet that he'd suddenly gotten so shy.

"It's hard, what I want to say."

"Come on, Darnell," Marnyke cooed.

He took a sip of water. "Marnyke?"

"Yeah?"

"Is it okay if we don't go to prom together?"

What?

He had to be joking. That was it. The thing to do was to play along.

"Sure!" Marnyke said with a laugh. "I won' go with you. We don't even have to be boyfriend and girlfriend no mo'. You goin' to college. We'll find new peeps. How'll that be?"

Darnell looked visibly relieved. "Mar, you the best. I can't believe you been thinkin' in that direction too. Thank you so much for sayin' that. Thank you so, so much."

Marnyke felt like Mike Tyson had just hit her upside the head.

"You serious, Darnell?"

"You know I am," he told her. "I'm thinkin' maybe the best thing for us to do is break up. Right here, right now."

CHAPTER 3

"What? You think we should break up?" Marnyke exclaimed. She was shocked. More than shocked, actually. Shocked, confused, and sick to her stomach.

"Let's get real. I'm goin' to Long Beach. I gotta go next month, actually, for remedial English. I'll be there; you be here. You know those things don't never work."

"We don't know that!" Marnyke said hotly.

"They don't," he said flatly. "Someone always get hurt. This way, we wrap up good an' stay friends. Whatchu say, Marnyke? Whatchu think?"

What did Marnyke think? A lot of things. All of them had to do with Darnell, and all of them started with the letters—

He couldn't be serious.

"Come on, Darnell," she told him softly. "Don't be like this. I ... I love you."

There. She'd said the words she'd never said to anyone before. She hoped they would restore him to sanity. They could have a good laugh and pretend the last two minutes hadn't ever happened.

"Can't we break up after prom?" Marnyke continued desperately.

Darnell shook his head. "Nah, I'd feel like a fraud."

"Darnell, I'm beggin' you! Do it fo' me!"

He shook his head.

Marnyke felt hot blood rush to her face. She'd just begged. Darnell had turned her down.

Well, two can play that game.

"Know what, Darnell?" Marnyke asked, her voice loud enough for others to hear. "This be what you want? Then I get to do what I want. An' what I want to do is this!"

Without warning, Marnyke picked up her glass and flung the icy water right in Darnell's face.

"Marnyke! Where you going?"

As she strode across the dining floor with soaked and stunned Darnell still at the table, Akira ran over to her. Marnyke started to sob right there in the center of the restaurant.

"He dumpin' me! I thought he was gonna ask me to prom, but now he dumpin' me!"

Wordlessly, Akira led her to a side room that was used for coatroom overflow and closed the door.

"Tell me everything," Akira urged.

Marnyke did.

When she was done, Akira shook her head. "I had no idea."

"I ain't blamin' you!" Marnyke wailed through her sniffles. Her sister handed her tissues; she blew her nose and dabbed at her reddened eyes.

"I don't even want you to think in that direction," Akira assured her. "When Darnell called, I thought it was so he could ask you to prom someplace special. Not this."

"Why he do it here?" Marnyke moaned.

"I guess he thought you wouldn't make a scene," Akira pronounced.

"He thought wrong." Marnyke blew her nose again and then threw the tissues away. "What am I gonna do? Everybody gonna laugh at me!"

"No one's gonna laugh," her sister disagreed. "They gonna laugh at yo' sorry-ass ex-boyfriend."

"You don't know Tia Ramirez. Or even Sherise Butler. They gonna be all happy that Darnell wrecked my life!"

"Marnyke, this is only gonna wreck your life if you let it."

Marnyke snorted. "Cross-stitch that on a pillow."

"I don't cross-stitch," Akira said.

"An' I don't have a date for the prom," Marnyke lamented.

Akira rubbed her chin thoughtfully. "I might be able to do something about that."

"I don't care about another prom date!" Marnyke looked her sister in the eye. "You got any more water? 'Cause I ain't done with Darnell."

CHAPTER 4

Marnyke dreaded going to school the next day, Tuesday.

It turned out to be worse than she thought.

From the moment she went through the metal detectors at South Central High School and started toward her locker, the comments flew. Some were from kids she didn't even know.

"Yo, Marnyke! How it feel to be dumped by the big D?"

"Yo, yo, yo, Marnyke. You need a date to the prom? My dog be available!"

Marnyke had a personal motto. "When you feel your worst, look your best." That morning, she'd put on black boots, tight black pants, a white camisole, a see-through chiffon top plus a black choker and big hoop earrings. As the comments and barbs continued to fly, the nice outfit didn't make her feel any better.

"Marnyke! You not lookin' so good!"

"Yo, yo, yo, Marnyke!"

The night before, she'd texted Kiki about her breakup. Kiki was the opposite of a gossip, which meant someone else had spread the word of what had happened.

Obviously, Darnell had run his mouth. She hated him for that maybe most of all.

South Central High School was an old school. The floors were battered linoleum. The walls and ceilings were made of cinderblocks. The shouts and laughter of a thousand kids arriving in the morning was deafening.

"Hey, Marnyke! Wassup!"

A guy from her science class stepped in front of her as she neared her locker. He was short and had a sad case of zits.

What's his name again? Terrence? Lawrence? Terrence.

"Hi, Terrence," she said wearily.

"Hey." Terrence wore jeans and a long-sleeve T-shirt. He shifted uncomfortably. "So, I heard what happened with Darnell."

"Who tol' you?" Marnyke demanded.

Terrence waved vaguely in the direction of some other kids. "Everyone knows. So, Marnyke, I always thought you were extra-fine. I mean, a stone fox, you know what I'm sayin'? So what you think about goin' to the prom with me? I wasn't plannin' to go, but now that Darnell—"

"Sorry, Terrence. I ain't goin' to prom with you."

God. He's like the last person I'd—

"Hey, Marnyke! You lookin' fine!"

Jackson's buddy Lattrell approached her. He was a shorter, less funny version of Jackson in baggy pants, basketball kicks, and a white T-shirt under a baggy flannel shirt. Marnyke had never had a real convo with him.

Obviously, that was about to change.

"Hey, Lattrell." She kept walking, heels clicking on the linoleum as she headed for her locker. There were only a few minutes before English with Ms. O.

"I heard what happened with Darnell."

"I think the whole world done heard." Marnyke reached her locker and spun the lock dial.

"You got a date for prom? 'Cause if you wanna go with me, I'm good with that."

Marnyke opened her locker, grabbed her English textbook, and slammed the locker shut.

"Lattrell, whatsa matter with you? I don't know you, an' I don't really care to know you. An' if I did know you, I'd never go to prom with a guy who says, ' 'Cause if you wanna go with me, I'm good wit' that.' What girl wants to go wit' a guy who be 'good wit' that'? Say somethin' to make her want to go with you!"

Lattrell grinned sheepishly. "I guess that means no."

"That's right, Lattrell. No. No. No!"

Marnyke stormed down the hall. Kiki thankfully caught up to her. She was dressed in typical Kiki gear: jeans and a basketball shirt. Her hair was in her usual braids, and she wore no makeup.

"I saw that with Lattrell," Kiki told her. "Every boy in the school gonna be hitting on you."

Marnyke sighed. This was a day that couldn't get any worse. In the coatroom at Citron, Akira had said she could help with a prom date. Marnyke hadn't given it any thought then, but she told her sister later that she'd accept her help. Now she wondered if it would be better to say yes to some harmless guy from school. She wouldn't have to kiss him, just go with him. It would make things so much—

"Marnyke and Kiki! Well, well. What a surprise!"

Tia Ramirez. Arm in arm with Ty Kessler. Hanging on Ty, in fact, like they were superglued. Tia wore white shorts and blue polo shirt, while Ty was in black pants and a paisley shirt.

"Why don't you git your butt to class, Tia?" Kiki asked.

"Why don't you two go to prom together?" Tia shot back. "You could be prom queen and prom queen!"

Marnyke seethed. Meanwhile, Ty cracked up.

"I have a date already, for yo' information," Kiki retorted. "An' Marnyke would have had a date too if her ex wasn't such a loser."

Tia smiled evilly. "Maybe Darnell just got smart."

"Tia, get yo' Latina ass outta here 'fore I get it outta here for you," Marnyke warned.

"What are you going to do, hit me?" Tia challenged.

"If I have to," Marnyke growled.

The two girls glared at each other. If it had gone another five seconds, Marnyke might have slugged her. But a raspy male voice got her attention.

"Marnyke Cooper! May I see you for a moment?"

Marnyke turned around. She knew she was gonna see Mr. Crandall. Almost sixty years old, with thinning hair veering toward gray and watery eyes, their alleged guidance counselor wore his Tuesday suit—threadbare gray with a white shirt and too-wide green tie. "You other kids, get to first period! Marnyke, stay with me."

The bell rang; Marnyke wondered what this was about. She'd been coming to school regularly for weeks. She was okay in all her classes too.

" 'Cept for English," she reminded herself. "I'm hangin' on by a thread."

"You have an academic problem, Marnyke," Crandall finally said.

"I'm passing everything!" Marnyke defended.

"You were passing everything," Crandall said, "until I took a look at your records. Ms. Okoro gave you credit for makeup work you did for days where you had an unexcused absence. Those grades will be changed to zero. With those zeros, you are on track to fail."

Marnyke stood there, mute and stunned. Crandall was changing grades that Ms. O had already given her? There had to be some kind of rule against that.

It was like the guidance counselor anticipated her thought.

"It's all legal," Crandall said mildly. "I checked with the district. In fact, Ms. Okoro is being reprimanded."

"I need to pass that class!" Marnyke declared.

"Very true," Crandall agreed. "Or else you'll be held back. The deadline for summer school registration has passed. Pity. Alas, there are no more graded assignments in your class this year. More pity."

No more assignments? Then I'm so messed up, it ain't funny.

"However, there might be a solution," Crandall went on.

"What's that?"

"I have the discretion to administer an additional assignment." Crandall resettled his glasses on his nose. "If you're willing to do it."

Marnyke was desperate. She did not want to be held back. "What's the assignment?" she sighed.

"I've talked to all your teachers," Crandall told her. "You are an exceptionally poor writer. However, if you can write an acceptable five paragraph essay on a subject of my choosing, you can earn a passing grade. Acceptable means a grade of A or B."

Marnyke's heart sunk. Crandall was right. She was a bad writer. She hated to write. Essays had been her downfall for years. She'd rather get her teeth drilled without Novocain than write an essay.

Now she had to do a private one for Crandall?

Crandall's eyes bore into hers. "Five paragraphs. Handwritten. Under my supervision in my office, so there will be no chance to cheat. Graded by myself and Ms. Okoro, respectively. Understood?"

"Yes, sir," Marnyke said softly. *He's setting me up. He probably heard what happened with Darnell, an' this be his way of rubbing it in.*

"You'll do it?" Crandall asked. "Oh yes. I almost forgot. If you don't pass English, forget prom. No matter who—if anyone!—invites you."

"I'll do it," she muttered.

Crandall didn't say anything else. He just walked away, leaving Marnyke alone in the empty hallway.

She'd thought the day couldn't get any worse. It just had.

CHAPTER 5

Later that afternoon, Marnyke let herself into the apartment on Jarvis Avenue that she shared with her sister. Their building was part of a block that was made to look like a street of regular apartment buildings, but it was owned by the city just the same. They were on the sixth floor, and there was no elevator. Climbing the stairs in heels was a real pain.

The apartment was small. "A shotgun," Marnyke always said, meaning you could shoot a shotgun from the front door at one end and the pellets would fly out the bedroom window at the other end. They had a kitchen, living room, small bathroom, and one bedroom that they'd divided into two halves. All the furniture was secondhand.

As she stepped inside, she heard Akira on the phone in the living room. She kicked off her boots, put down her books, and tried to figure out who Akira—who wore sweat pants and a black bra—was talking to.

When she figured it out, her heart sunk.

"Mid-July—Got it—Uh-huh—Uh-huh—Uh-huh—You doin' any training for a job? You learnin' any skills?—Uh-huh."

"You talkin' to Mama?" Marnyke asked.

Akira held up a hand to shush Marnyke. "Uh-huh—Yeah, she right here with me. You want to say hello?"

Akira passed her cell to Marnyke. For the longest time they had a landline so that they could get collect calls from their mother up at the women's prison in Sandersville. Then they found this company that helped them get collect calls on Akira's cell.

Marnyke didn't really want to talk. Life had actually improved after her mother was sent away.

But still, a mother was a mother was a mother.

"Hi, Mama," she said.

"Babygirl! It's your mama, and I got some great news!" Marnyke heard the familiar beep; the call beeped every fifteen seconds to remind them that they were being recorded. "I'm gettin' released! Your mama be comin' home!"

Coming home? She isn't supposed to be released for eighteen mo' months!

"That's ... that's big news, Mama. When?"

"July. I'll be home for yo' sister's wedding! I'm getting time off for bein' such a good girl! Your mama is coming home. Ain't it gonna be great?"

Marnyke gulped. "Yeah, Mama. Great."

"Well, your mama's gotta go now," her mother said. "But I'll be callin' again soon. We got so much to figure out! Bye. You be good, Babygirl!"

"I hate when she calls me Babygirl," Marnyke thought as she gave the phone back to Akira. "She didn't treat me good as a baby, an' she didn't treat me good as a girl."

"She be home for your wedding. She gonna embarrass us," Marnyke said sourly. "What we gonna do?"

"I don't know."

"You're getting married to Ashon. You told me I could keep the apartment;

that you guys were gonna get a place nearby." Marnyke's voice cracked with emotion. "I don't want to live with her. I can't stand that I'm sayin' that, but it's true."

Marnyke felt terrible at what she'd just said, but their mother was a bad influence. She remembered coming home to find her passed out in the hallway or sleeping in a puddle of her own vomit.

No. I can't live like that again.

"I gotta think about all this," Akira declared.

"You and me both."

"We got a little time." Her sister stood and rubbed her temples. "Talking to her gives me a headache."

"Well, livin' with her gonna give me a bigger headache!"

Marnyke went into the kitchen and filled a coffee cup with water. She drank it down and felt guilty for having just yelled at Akira. It wasn't Akira's fault that their mom was getting out of Sandersville much sooner than they'd expected.

"How was your day?" Akira asked when Marnyke came back to the living room.

"It blew," Marnyke admitted. She sat down on an old beanbag sack they'd scavenged and told her sister how everyone had acted about Darnell and what Crandall had said about her English grade.

"Can't help with the English," Akira told her.

"What about prom?"

Akira smiled. "You still want me to help you with a date?"

Marnyke shrugged. "Maybe I jus' won't go. That'd be the easiest thing."

"No need for that. Hold on."

Akira took out her phone and sent a quick text. "That's to Brodney."

"Who be Brodney?"

Marnyke got her answer a second later when she answered a rap on the door of their apartment. A tall, handsome young man with deep ebony skin, gleaming teeth, and flashing dark eyes stood there. He wore a gold V-neck sweater and broken-in tennis shoes. His smile was dazzling.

"Marnyke," Akira said, coming up behind her. "Meet Brodney Wells. Brodney's a freshman—well, he just finished freshman year—at Spellman College in Atlanta. He's a music major—jazz piano. He in town till next week visiting some relatives of Ashon's. That's how I met him."

Brodney put a hand out. "Good to meet you, Marnyke." The voice was as intoxicating as the smile.

"Nice to meet you, Brodney." She shook his hand.

Akira laughed. "Now that we got that out of the way, I think Brodney's got a question for you, Marnyke."

Brodney gazed into Marnyke's eyes. "Marnyke Cooper, it would be an honor for me to escort you to your school prom. Hold on. You don't even know me. If you let me come in, I can tell you a little about myself."

CHAPTER 6

"What about you, Marnyke?" Tia turned to her. Her eyes still glinted with thinly veiled joy that Darnell had dumped Marnyke. "You got someone to go with?"

"Yeah, Marnyke," Sherise chimed in. "We're all goin' on a field trip to the San Marino after school to check it out. But it seem like you be the one checkin' out."

"Mee-ow!" Nishell made an alley cat sound. "No claws in the cafeteria, please."

It was lunchtime the next day at South Central High School. As usual, the YC girls had taken over the table farthest from the food line. So far, Marnyke hadn't said a word to anyone—not even Kiki—about Brodney. It was going to be too delicious to see their faces when she announced she was coming to prom with a college man.

I'm gonna turn it out and watch them get all twisted.

"Marnyke still gotta pass English before she can even go," Tia reminded everyone.

Word about Marnyke's problems with Mr. Crandall had spread as fast as the news that Darnell had dumped her.

"I'll pass English," Marnyke said with more confidence than she felt. She hadn't done nearly enough to prepare for Crandall's essay, and she knew it.

"That still leaves you without no date," Sherise remarked, twirling her hair.

"Lattrell's available," Tia cracked. "And so is Terrence."

"I don't think so," Marnyke said lightly.

"Whatchu mean?" Sherise demanded. "You won' go wit' them, or you mean you got a date?"

Now's the time. Milk it, baby. Milk it good.

"Brodney," Marnyke said with a light smile.

"Brodney? Who's Brodney?" Tia demanded.

"You know anyone named Brodney?" Sherise asked Nishell and Kiki.

Marnyke saw Nishell and Kiki shake their heads and grin. Kiki was her bestie. Nishell had gotten a lot friendlier these last couple of months. She loved that they were supporting her.

"Who say he even go to our school?" Marnyke said, smiling a bit more.

"He goes to another high school?" Tia asked hotly.

Marnyke sighed. "Tia, let me 'splain it to you like a six year old so that I only have to do it once. His name be Brodney Wells. He goes to Spellman down in the ATL, which is a college you'll never get into. He finishin' freshman year, and he a music major. He play jazz piano. He tall, he smart, and he fine. Compared to Brodney, Darnell be a scrub!"

Marnyke finished with a flourish, enjoying the shocked looks on both Tia and Sherise's face.

Just then, Darnell walked past their table. He seemed to want to say something. Marnyke knew if she gave him any encouragement at all, he might. So she just turned and looked out the window. Darnell stepped away.

"You're a stone-cold bee-yotch, Marnyke," Tia scolded.

"Tia, he dropped me. He got to deal with it."

"You got a pic of this Brodney?" Sherise demanded.

If Marnyke had thought to take a cell phone picture of him, she would have. But she hadn't.

Damn.

"You'll see him at prom, Sherise," she promised. "And you gonna wish he was your date 'stead of Carlos."

Tia wasn't done. "How'd you get him to ask you so fast?"

Marnyke had enough of twenty questions. Plus, she'd had exactly one conversation with Brodney. He'd shared a bit about his life, but it would suck to be nailed by questions she couldn't answer.

"I got him to ask me 'cause he know quality when he see it," she told them. "Now, 'scuse me, bee-yotches. I'll see you at the San Marino. Right now, I got me some English to study for."

"Welcome to the Hotel San Marino! My name is Mary Anne Mackey, and I'll be your guide. It's wonderful to have you young ladies with us."

Marnyke and the other YC girls stood together in a cluster in the immense marble lobby of the Hotel San Marino. Their tour was about to start with Mary Anne as their guide. Everything about Mary Anne was perky. Perky blond hair. Perky makeup. Perky black heels. Perky blue skirt and white shirt. Perky upturned nose.

"If she was any mo' perky," Marnyke thought sourly, "her last name would be Perkins."

Still, Marnyke was impressed. The hotel took up three square blocks of the city's financial district. There were ten glass doors—Marnyke had counted them—with at least that many uniformed doormen. The lobby seemed as big as a football field, all in white marble, with museum-quality sculptures, fountains, and a white grand piano. To the left was a cozy bar with soft jazz playing. To the right was the bell station, where uniformed bellmen stood ready to whisk arriving guests' luggage up to their rooms.

The lobby teemed with people. Asian, East Indian, African, African American—it was like a super-rich version of the United Nations. Super-rich for sure, since Mary Anne explained that the average nightly room rate was six hundred dollars.

"Big Boss was hoping to join us," the tour guide told them, "but he called to say he's stuck at the shop. He did want you to know that he's taking care of everything."

Nishell raised her hand politely. She had her camera around her neck. "We'll still need to take pictures, though. For next year's yearbook."

Mary Anne laughed. "No, you won't. There'll be three professional photographers. All you girls have to do is have fun. Now, it's time for our tour. Follow me."

The girls were psyched as Mary Anne led them perkily through the lobby. Marnyke pushed aside any thoughts of the English essay so she could enjoy the experience.

The tour made Marnyke want to get super-rich quick.

They saw the full-service spa and hair salon, the hotel bowling alley, the nightclub, the four restaurants, the ground floor meditation garden, the rooftop pool, and even the suite where the Obamas had stayed when they'd come to town.

Mary Anne saved the Excelsior Ballroom for last. "It's worth the wait," she promised as she led them back through the lobby. "We have six ballrooms. The Excelsior is my favorite."

They traipsed through the lobby, and then down a long, wide corridor.

"Here we are," Mary Anne announced when they reached the Excelsior. "Mind you, it's empty. But our crew will decorate it. Big Boss asked for a yearbook theme. Okay, here we go."

Mary Anne opened the door. The girls stepped inside.

Oh. My. God.

The ballroom was three times as big as the lobby. The ceiling seemed like it was a hundred feet high. There was a full-sized stage at one end. Though empty, the walls were covered in thousands of tiny white bulbs that blinked like summer fireflies by the river.

"Wow," Marnyke breathed aloud.

"You like?" Mary Anne asked. "Big Boss is bringing in a band *and* a deejay.

You won't have heard of the band, but he says they're wonderful."

Everyone nodded. Marnyke tried to picture how this ballroom would be decked out for prom. She couldn't. It was too big.

They filed out in a happy daze. To Marnyke's surprise, just before they left the ballroom, Kiki pulled her to one side. She looked oddly worried.

"What's wrong, homegirl?" Marnyke asked her. "You should be all happy and whatnot. We be tickin' and struttin' and wavin' right in this room come Saturday. Look at this place!"

Kiki's eyes narrowed. "I should be all happy, yeah. But I'm not. Marnyke, I need help. An' you the only one who can help me!"

CHAPTER 7

"I cannot believe you makin' me do this," Kiki muttered through gritted teeth.

"You wanna be a hot girl, don't chu?" Marnyke retorted. "You wanna be fly? You wanna be all that?"

"Yeah. But—"

"Then do as I say or do it on your own," Marnyke said.

Though she was face up on a massage table, Kiki seemed to melt. "Okay. Jus' get this over with."

LaQueesha—the very tall, very wide eyelash tech who was about to work on

Kiki's lashes—harrumphed with irritation. She turned to Marnyke. "Fo' how fast we put this together for yo' friend, she should be washin' our feet and singin'."

"I don't sing, and I don' wash no one's feet but my own!" Kiki protested.

"Then hold yo' black tush still," LaQueesha ordered. She checked the buttons on her blue smock then stood over Kiki and leaned in, grasping a single false eyelash with tweezers in one hand and little tube of glue in the other. "I don' want to glue yo' eyes shut."

It was the next afternoon after school. There were just two days before prom. At the hotel, Kiki had spoken to Marnyke from her heart.

"I should be all happy, yeah. But I'm not. Marnyke, I need help. You the only one who can help me! I want to be a hot girl for Sean. Can you help me, Marnyke? An' I don't got no money to spend!"

Right there in the ballroom, Marnyke had taken Kiki by the shoulders and looked into her scared dark eyes.

"Girlfriend, you done come to the right place."

Marnyke was a so-so student and a so-so athlete. She was not like Kiki, who was a total brain and one of the best girl basketball players in the city. That said, no one in the whole damn school was better than Marnyke at looking good on a budget. If anyone could turn gawky Kiki Butler into a hot girl for one night, it was Marnyke.

On the bus ride home from the San Marino, Marnyke had started calling in favors.

First call was to Eastside Beauty School. Marnyke modeled there on many Saturdays, letting the students practice on her face, hair, and nails. A quick convo with Mrs. Charles, the boss, got Kiki hooked up for free hair styling, makeup, eyelashes, and a custom mani-pedi.

Next call was to her favorite used clothing store in the Korean part of town. Before coming to the beauty school, Marnyke stopped in to pick her friend a gown. The owner, Ji Min Kim, said there'd be no charge to rent it for the weekend since Marnyke was such a good customer. Marnyke also chose a handbag, heels, and jewelry for her friend.

Marnyke smiled as she watched LaQueesha do her thing. Kiki had great eyebrows and wonderful almond-shaped eyes. Her natural lashes, though, were lame. LaQueesha glued on fake lashes, one by one.

"Gimme a mirror," Kiki growled when LaQueesha was done.

Marnyke shook her head. "No, girl. Not till you're all done."

Kiki sat up; LaQueesha helped her off the table. "Now Mrs. Charles gonna do something 'bout those braids. Who you think you is? Solange?"

"Who Mrs. Charles?" Kiki asked suspiciously.

"She runs the beauty school," Marnyke told her.

LaQueesha frowned at Kiki. "You ain't goin' to prom dressed like that, are you?"

Kiki had come to the shop dressed in cutoffs and one of her basketball jerseys. "Just let's get my hair done."

Marnyke laughed. It was fun to see Kiki so out of her element.

Mrs. Charles—a chunky, no-nonsense lady in her fifties who wore the same blue smock as her students—did Kiki's hair and makeup in front of a beauty school class. With plenty of commentary to the students, she took out the braids, washed Kiki's hair, and then straightened, cut, and styled it to fall rakishly over Kiki's right eye. Next, she shaped Kiki's eyebrows to form an extra high arch.

Lastly, she taught the students how to do dramatic makeup for a formal party. She used foundation with plum undertones to match Kiki's skin tone. Then she applied glittery eye liner and added mascara to Kiki's new eyelashes. She finished with plum lipstick on Kiki's soft lips.

When she was done, the class clapped and cheered.

"Can I see now?" Kiki asked.

Marnyke picked up a different tone in Kiki's voice now. Excitement.

"Nope," Marnyke said. "Go in the dressing room. Your gown and shoes in there. I covered all the mirrors. No peeking!"

Kiki went to change. A few minutes later, she emerged.

There were audible gasps.

"Do I look okay?" Kiki asked shyly.

Marnyke wanted to cry—tears of joy, that is. As the students and Mrs. Charles followed, Marnyke walked Kiki to a three-quarter-around standing mirror.

"Close your eyes till I say so," she told her friend.

Kiki did as she was told until Marnyke had her perfectly positioned.

"Open!" Marnyke ordered.

Kiki looked. "Oh. Oh, oh, oh!"

She was beautiful.

The dress was classic black with a high neckline—Kiki didn't have much on top—and a plunging back that showed off her well-shaped lats. It was tight in the booty and fell in shapely folds to mid-thigh. The heels were three-inchers and patent leather.

Kiki laughed with glee. "Day-um! I'm hot!"

"You a beautiful girl," Marnyke told her. "You gonna break hearts Saturday night."

A boy called out from the back of the throng. "She already breakin' mine!"

"True enough," Marnyke said with a grin. "Kiki, get changed and put the dress back in the garment bag. An' wash yo' face. We got one mo' stop 'fore we go home."

"You're sure this okay wit' your girlfriend?" Kiki was disbelieving.

Brodney nodded. "It's fine. I checked."

Marnyke raised her eyebrows at Kiki. "I tol' you!"

Brodney offered Kiki his cell phone. "You want to call? She's number one on my speed dial."

It was a half hour later. Marnyke, Kiki, and Brodney were sitting together at an outdoor café in Riverfront Park. Not really a café. Just a few plastic tables and chairs and a food truck that served snacks, coffee, and drinks. They'd gotten sodas and were sharing a few orders of fries. Brodney had come down to meet them at Marnyke's request. Marnyke wanted her bestie to meet her date before prom.

"You sayin' it's fine if I call her," Kiki declared skeptically.

"Gimme the phone," Brodney said with a laugh. He looked great in black jeans and another one of his V-necks—this time with a plaid shirt over it. "I'm puttin' her on speaker. Her name is Alicia."

He pressed the touch screen; Marnyke heard a ring and a pickup.

"Hey, baby." Alicia's voice was sweet and friendly. "How's the big city treatin' you?"

"Hey," Brodney said easily. "I'm here with Marnyke—I told you about her—

and her friend Kiki, and we got you on speaker. I'm good to go to prom with Marnyke, right?"

Alicia laughed. "It's all good. The way that boy—what was his name, Darnell?—treated her, you can pretend to be her boyfriend if that's what Marnyke wants. You hear me, Marnyke? It's fine with me!"

Brodney had told Marnyke this when they met on Tuesday. Still, Marnyke felt great to hear it from the girl herself.

"Okay, baby," Brodney said. "I'm gonna go."

"Call me later."

"You know it. I love you."

Brodney clicked off. Marnyke was touched by their obvious connection.

Darnell never talked to me that way. Not even once.

"She's a great girl," Brodney said. "English major. Already on the Spellman literary magazine. She's gonna be a big writer some day. Mark my words."

"I could use a writer tomorrow," Marnyke muttered.

"With what?" Brodney asked.

She quickly told him about the essay she had to write the next day in Crandall's office. He actually got a little mad.

"Why didn't you tell me? Did she tell you?" He looked at Kiki.

Kiki nodded. "Uh-huh. I'm jus' waiting for her to get serious."

Brodney's eyes blazed as they swung toward Marnyke. "Waitin' to get serious? It's tomorrow!"

Marnyke's face burned. She knew she'd done little to prep for the essay.

She realized that she was hoping it would just go away.

Brodney took charge. "You're good in school, Kiki?"

Kiki nodded.

"Then help me out," he ordered. Then he refocused on Marnyke. "I got ninety minutes to teach you to write a five paragraph essay. I just hope it's enough time."

CHAPTER 8

Ninety minutes later, they were still at it. The drinks were largely untouched; the fries cold and uneaten.

"What's the most important thing to remember when you first get the topic?" Brodney asked.

Marnyke sighed. Brodney and Kiki had been pounding her for an hour and a half about the right way to write a five paragraph essay. She realized it was the same thing that Ms. O had been saying all year, but she'd never really paid enough attention.

"Answer the question. Then prove my case."

"How you do that?" Kiki demanded.

"Examples."

"And how you tell the teacher, 'Yo! Listen up! What be comin' up right here be an example?' " Kiki pressed.

"I write, 'For example, blah blah blah.' Or I write, 'You can also see this in blah blah blah.' " Marnyke told them. "Or I say, 'Another illustration be blah—' "

"Another illustration is! Not another illustration be! Another illustration is!" Brodney banged his hand on the table, making the drinks shake dangerously. "Proper English when you're writing. That just how it be."

The three of them looked at each other for a moment and laughed.

"That be wack," Marnyke thought. "How you talk in real life can't be how you write in real life? But as Brodney say, that just how it be."

Marnyke nodded wearily. "I got it."

"I think you have," Brodney said gently. "So I'll repeat it just once more. Lots of examples, lots of 'for instances,' and keep your sentences short to stay out of trouble. If a sentence has more than fifteen words, it's too long. You're writing a five paragraph essay, not some John Edgar Wideman book. And don't be afraid. Be brave."

Marnyke took a long swallow of her tepid Coke. "Thank you. You should be a teacher."

"If the music thing don't work out, maybe I will." Brodney stood and closed the buttons on his plaid shirt. It had cooled as evening approached. "Okay, I gotta bounce. Marnyke, I'll call you. Kiki, I'll see you Saturday night."

He hugged both girls and then took off. A few minutes later, Marnyke and Kiki headed out too. Kiki carried a shopping bag with her shoes and accessories in one hand and a black garment bag with her prom gown in the other. Before they separated to find their buses, Marnyke thanked her friend and told her she was beautiful. Kiki batted her new eyelashes and grinned.

"I ain't never gonna keep it up after prom," she told Marnyke.

"Never say never."

Marnyke's bus came quickly; she got to Jarvis Avenue in twenty minutes. Night was falling. Marnyke didn't like to be alone on the street after dark. It wasn't safe for a girl. She hurried to her building.

She'd just started up the five stone steps to the door of her building when she heard a male voice call.

"Marnyke!"

She turned. There was Darnell, a few steps behind her. He wore Nike kicks, baggy green Celtics shorts, a yellow T-shirt, and carried a basketball.

"Can we talk?" he asked. "I know if I called you, you wouldn't answer. So I came to see you. I been waitin' since four."

Marnyke bit her lower lip. She really didn't want to get into a scene with Darnell. He'd dropped her. Couldn't he just leave it be?

"Please?" he asked again.

She sighed. He had been waiting a long time.

"Okay," Marnyke decided. "Five minutes. That's it."

"That's all I need."

Darnell scrambled up the stoop, found a couple of sheets of cardboard, and gave one to Marnyke to sit on. They plopped down side by side. She didn't want him to touch her. She didn't trust herself. Darnell was so fine—

"I done wrong at that restaurant," he declared.

She frowned. "You think, Darnell?"

He turned to her, ochre light from a street lamp glinting off his forehead. "Done wrong. I want to say I'm sorry. I was sorry right away, in fact."

Marnyke put a hand to her cheek— the same cheek Darnell used to touch. What he was saying sounded sincere. But it didn't erase what had happened. She looked into her heart. She didn't love him now.

"'Pology accepted," she told him. "You got anything else to say?"

He bristled. "Why you gotta be like that? All distant and bull—"

"You dumped me, Darnell!" Marnyke shot back. "You may be sorry, but you still did it. Why didn't you call me that night if you felt so bad?"

His voice got strained. "I made a mistake. Ain't chu ever made a mistake?"

"I made plenty," Marnyke admitted.

"Well then." He folded his arms across his chest defiantly.

Marnyke folded her arms too. "But I never dumped someone like you did me!"

They sat in silence for a few minutes, though it never really got quiet in midtown. Cars rolled. Hip-hop spilled from open windows. Ambulances keened; ghetto birds cut through the sky overhead, their blades whirring angrily.

"Who the guy?" Darnell asked.

"What?"

"Who be the guy? I hear you goin' to prom with some dude from the ATL."

Marnyke stared into the night. "Is that what this is about?"

"Who he be?" Darnell demanded.

"His name be Brodney, an' it ain't none of your beeswax!"

"If he goin' with you, Marnyke, it my business," Darnell retorted. "How you meet him?"

Marnyke stood. It was one thing to have a jealous boyfriend. It was another to have a jealous ex. She didn't have to put up with Darnell's crap for one more second.

"You better recognize, Darnell. We done here," she told him.

"Answer my question!" he ordered, bouncing to his feet.

"Darnell, all I can say 'bout Brodney is that he showin' me a different way a man can be. An' I like it. Goodnight and good-bye."

"I'm gonna be there, you know!" he challenged.

"You do whatchu want," she answered coldly.

She marched inside, hit the stairs, and let herself into the apartment. Since Akira was at work, the place was dark. Even before she turned on a light, she tried to imagine what it would be like to come home to an apartment with no Akira but her mama.

I could be findin' Mama here dead drunk on the kitchen floor.

Her cell rang before she could ponder that thought.

It was Tia. Marnyke really didn't want to talk to her. Still, she answered.

"Yeah?"

"It's me, Tia," Tia said.

"And me." Marnyke was surprised to hear Nishell's voice too.

"And me!" Sherise chirped. "We on three-way."

What the hell?

Nishell spoke next. "We saw Kiki's hair!"

"It's the bomb!" Sherise declared.

"And the gown! Sherise sent us a picture," Tia added.

Sherise whistled so loud that Marnyke had to move her cell away from her ear. "And Kiki told us 'bout her makeup!"

There was only one thing Marnyke could say to all these compliments. "Thank you."

"Nishell, you're going to ask her, right?" Tia prompted.

Still in the dark, Marnyke plopped down on the living room couch. "Ask what?"

"Well ..." Nishell hesitated. "We got prom gowns and all, but we was wonderin' ... what you did for Kiki, could you do for us? We wan' our men to go, 'Wow!' when they see us."

"Please?" Sherise asked.

"Double please?" Tia chimed in.

Marnyke was stunned. Here were three girls—two of whom she didn't like all that much—pleading for help. She could have been irritated, but that's not what she felt.

She felt valuable. Needed. Special.

"Okay," she told them. "We got a date after school tomorrow. You bee-yotches gonna look better than you ever looked in your life!"

CHAPTER 9

Marnyke was waiting nervously in Mr. Crandall's office when the guidance counselor stepped inside. He wore a gray suit, black collared shirt, and white tie. His dishwater hair was disheveled; his wire-rim glasses dirty.

Day-um. He look old.

There was no time to think about that, though. Or about the cheesy framed pictures of birds that decorated Crandall's office walls. The guidance counselor stiffly handed her a sealed manila envelope and then started yammering a mile a minute. The more he said, the more worried Marnyke got.

"This is your essay assignment," Crandall barked. "You will open the envelope. You will read the question inside this envelope. There is scratch paper and lined paper for your essay. You will write on the lined paper or you will fail. If you do not answer the question, you will fail. You will write five paragraphs. If it is not precisely five paragraphs, you will fail. It will be graded by Ms. Okoro and me, separately, as soon as you are finished. If either of us gives you less than a B, you will fail. Questions?"

Yes. Crandall, it be my imagination or is you settin' me up to fail?

Stone-faced, she shook her head.

Crandall went and sat behind his desk, put his feet up, and took out a teachers' union magazine. "I'm staying so you won't even think of using your cell phone for help." He checked his old-fashioned wristwatch. "You have forty-five minutes. Begin."

Marnyke tore open the envelope, her heart beating crazily as she pulled out the contents. The question was on a single sheet of blue-tinted paper. All caps.

ESSAY QUESTION: DISCUSS AN IMPORTANT DECISION IN YOUR OWN LIFE AND WHOM IT WILL AFFECT.

That was it.

Precious time clicked off Crandall's digital wall clock as she scrambled for something to write. She was coming up with nothing.

She snuck a glance at Crandall. He eyeballed her, a sadistic smile working at his lips.

He enjoyin' this. He really do want me to fail. Well, that be too bad. I'm gonna break his old heart. If he even has a heart. I bet his heart made of steel.

That's it!

The idea of what to write had just smacked her like the clang of a steel prison cell door.

She could hear Brodney and Kiki's voices in her head as she scrawled a few notes about her introduction and conclusion. Then she outlined the topics of her three body paragraphs, writing a few words about the examples she'd use in each of them. Three per paragraph.

She glanced at the clock again. Thirty-nine minutes to go. She could take almost seven minutes on each paragraph and still have time to read it through at the end. She didn't have to panic. She had an outline now.

Short sentences. Examples. Be brave.

Marnyke wrote solidly for thirty-four minutes. Then she read her essay from start to finish.

The Hardest Decision

Every teenage boy or girl has hard decisions to make. Sometimes that decision is about school. Sometimes that decision is about what to do after school is done. Does the student want to go to college? Does the student want to go to work? Does the student want to go into the military? There are decisions about where to live and how to earn a living. There are decisions about boyfriends and girlfriends. I have all these decisions to make too, but I have an even harder decision to consider. Unlike most teenagers' mothers, my mother is going to be released from jail in two months. I now live with my sister, Akira, but she is getting married this summer. I have to decide what to do when my mother is released. Do I live with my mother, or do I move out? My decision will affect my sister, my mother, and most of all, myself.

My decision will affect my sister. For example, if I decide to stay and live with my mother, my sister may feel anxious for me. Another illustration of how Akira will be affected is if I move out and live with a friend. Akira may feel I am quitting on my mother. One more way that my decision could affect Akira is that I might want to keep living with her. That would be good for me. It might be bad for her new marriage.

My decision will affect my mother. For instance, my mother may not be able to live on her own without help. If I am not there to help her, she might not survive well. Another way it will affect my mother is that my mother may think she can still boss me around. I am a lot older now than I was when she went to jail. I don't like the idea of her telling me what to do. One more example of how my decision will affect my mother has to do with how angry I am at her for going to jail. I am afraid that anger could carry over into life.

Most of all, the decision will affect me. First, I don't know who I will be loyal to the most. Will it be Akira, or will it be Mama? Second, I don't think my mother will be a very good role model. Without Akira, I don't know who will be my role model. Finally, I worry about whether I will have to act like a mother to my mother instead of like a daughter. It is hard enough to be her daughter.

In conclusion, I have a decision to make about my mother. It is a decision that will affect many people. It will most affect my mother, my sister, and me. I don't know what my decision is going to be. I understand how my choices will change the people I love and myself. All I can do is think about the factors and people I discuss in this essay. Then I will make the best decision I can.

Marnyke tapped her pen nervously against the paper. It wasn't perfect. Some sentences were too long. She wondered whether she should have made an actual decision and talked about it in the essay. It wasn't what the question called for, but what if that was what Crandall—

"Time!" Mr. Crandall practically leaped out of his chair toward Marnyke. "You wrote quite a bit."

"I guess so." Marnyke handed him her work.

"Wait here. Ms. Okoro and I are going to grade this now. It shouldn't take long."

Mr. Crandall left. Marnyke slumped in the seat. It was done. All she could do was wait and stare at those stupid bird drawings. One of the drawings was of a baby wren in a nest, crying for its mother. She tried to imagine what it would be like to want a mother that much.

Five minutes passed. Ten minutes.

At fifteen minutes after the hour, the door to his office opened. It wasn't Mr. Crandall, though. It was Ms. Okoro. She was in one of the long dresses that she'd brought with her when she came to America from Nigeria. This one was orange.

She looked solemn.

"Oh no," Marnyke thought. "It sucked. She hated it!"

Marnyke buried her face in her hands. Her stomach roiled. What was she going to do now? She wouldn't be allowed to go to prom; she'd be held back from—

"Here's your essay, Marnyke." Marnyke felt Ms. O put the essay on the desk.

Okay. Let's get this over with.

Marnyke took a deep breath and opened her eyes.

Omigod.

A. And next to it, B.

"The A is from me, Marnyke," Ms. O explained. "Mr. Crandall gave you a B. I do think he'd give a B to God, Marnyke. Don't tell him I said that. Congratulations, Marnyke. You did it!"

Omigod. Omigod. Omigod. I passed!

Marnyke whooped, punched the air, and started dancing around Mr. Crandall's office. Ms. O grinned at her. Then her teacher put her arms out. Marnyke went to her, tears of joy streaming down her face.

"You wrote a wonderful essay. Just wonderful. I had no idea about your mother," her teacher murmured.

"I never said nothin' to nobody," Marnyke admitted. "Till now."

"We can talk about her another time if you'd like. This essay proves you can do anything you set your mind to, Marnyke." Her chunky teacher continued to embrace her, and Marnyke's tears kept flowing. For having passed the essay. For what had happened with Darnell. For her mother.

"Yeah," Marnyke managed through her tears. "I guess I just did."

CHAPTER 10

Marnyke woke in her half-room on Saturday morning floating on a magic carpet of happiness. She checked her phone. Nine thirty in the morning. She'd slept for nine-and-a-half hours. Amazing.

Can life be better? I don't know how.

After she'd passed the essay test on Friday afternoon—Crandall never even stopped in to say congrats—she led the YC girls on a let's-get-slammin' expedition. Kiki came along, just for fun.

They started at Ji Min's store where she personally chose new prom gowns for Nishell, Sherise, and Tia. For Tia, Marnyke picked a sassy white silk gown that clung to Tia's behind for dear life, but also had a demure bow below a crisscross series of cutouts in back. Tia loved it.

For Sherise, Marnyke found a gray halter gown with the halter beaded in rhinestones. Worn with a pushup bra, there'd be plenty of cleavage; a spreading sunbeam of rhinestones stretching down and outward from the chest. Sherise had a gorgeous neck, so Marnyke found a choker that drew attention to it. The gown had a long slit up one leg; Sherise had great legs. Sherise strutted around in the gown like a runway model and said Carlos would have a hard time not wanting to take it off. Everyone loved it.

With mega-curvy Nishell, Marnyke went mega-sexy. She unearthed a light purple gown with a corset foundation that pulled in Nishell's tummy but still let her hips, booty, and plush chest do their thing. Dangerously low-cut, with gold filigreed between the low neckline and hips, the dress practically screamed, "Yo, world! Check out the hotness!"

At first, the gown was too much for Nishell until the other girls insisted she'd never looked better. Sherise cracked that she'd better give Jackson some sunglasses. Otherwise, he might go blind from looking at her.

Finally, Nishell loved it.

Ji Min told them all that since Marnyke was such an important customer, her friends could rent their dresses for the weekend for five dollars each. The girls gushed thanks to Ji Min and to Marnyke too. No way would this be happening without her.

After that, Marnyke took everyone to the beauty school for makeovers. By the time they were done, everyone had new 'dos and instructions on how to do their makeup, and Marnyke was a hero. Not only that, she felt like she'd just found her purpose in life.

Marnyke daydreamed as she rested her head on her gold pillow and stared up at the stained ceiling.

I can so see it on a business card. "Marnyke Cooper. Stylist to the Stars."

That night was prom. She'd be going with Brodney. One of the greatest things about it, Marnyke decided, was that Brodney had a girlfriend who Marnyke respected. Brodney was the kind of man—

Beep-beep!

Marnyke's cell sounded with an incoming call. That was a rarity. No one made actual calls anymore. Everyone texted.

She checked the number. Restricted.

"Hullo?" she answered.

"Hey, Marnyke. It's Brodney."

"Hey! I was jus' thinkin' 'bout you and how lucky Alicia be. Ready to tear it up tonight?"

"That's why I'm calling," Brodney said. His voice was oddly strained. "There's a problem."

"What kind of problem?" Marnyke swallowed hard.

Brodney gave a thin laugh. "This may sound nuts, but I'm at the urgent care place on Fourteenth Street."

Marnyke's first instinct was concern. "You hurt yourself?"

Again, there was the thin laugh. "I wish. I'd be better off. Marnyke, I just got diagnosed with chicken pox."

"You got the what?" Marnyke couldn't believe her ears.

"I've got chicken pox, Marnyke. Never had 'em as a kid; got 'em now. Doctor says I'm confined to quarters till I get better. Marnyke, I can't come to prom. I'm so sorry."

Oh no. Oh no, oh no.

Her thoughts came fast and furious.

Who's gonna be my date? If I show up alone, everyone'll say Brodney be a fake date from the start. They'll laugh at me.

Darnell gonna mock me.

"I'm so sorry," Brodney repeated.

Marnyke was about to share all these fears with Brodney but then decided to keep her mouth shut.

He helped so much with my essay. He wanted to help with prom. It ain't his fault he got sick. I ain't gonna make him feel worse.

"No worries," she told him, forcing her voice to stay light. "I got it covered. How about we meet up next week when you're better?"

"I'd like that," Brodney said with relief in his voice. "Alicia's actually comin' up to meet me on Monday. You'll get a chance to meet her if you want."

"To tell her how great her boyfriend be?" Marnyke laughed. "She already know!"

"I'll call when she gets here. How about that?"

"Word. Feel better, 'kay?"

They clicked off. With no need to fake it any more, Marnyke slumped into her pillow. Her prom date was gone. How was she ever going to find another one?

Fifteen minutes later, Marnyke was at the small kitchen table with Akira. They each wore T-shirts over panties, and they each drank their coffee the same way: black with one sugar. Marnyke had already shared her tale of woe with her sister. Now, she was spinning a crazy idea. "None of my friends ain't never seen Brodney," Marnyke related. " 'Cept for Kiki, and she be my bestie. She'll keep her mouth shut. What I'm thinkin'—I know it's nuts—is that if Brodney can't come to prom wit' me, I need someone who can pretend to be Brodney."

Akira shook her head. "It won't work. Ain't no way some guy can pretend to be Brodney."

"Let me worry 'bout that," Marnyke insisted, wrapping her hands around her chipped brown coffee cup. "Problem is, I don' know no one to ask."

Akira pursed her lips. "I have an idea. Maybe."

"Who?"

Her sister held up a single finger and took out her cell. First she called another waitress and asked for the number of someone named Devon.

"Who Devon?" Marnyke demanded.

Akira shushed her, jotted down the number, and then called the mystery guy. Like when her mother had called from prison, all Marnyke could do was listen in.

"Devon? It's Akira—Yes, from the restaurant. I need a favor, and I shared my tips with you big time, so you owe me—Uh-huh—Uh-huh—Well, my sister needs a prom date, and she needs you to pretend to be some college boy from Atlanta. You say you an actor. Can you do that?"

There was a long silence as Akira listened intently, and Marnyke's heart thudded.

"Uh-huh—Uh-huh—Uh-huh—You got a suit but no tux? That'll have to do. Meet her at the San Marino at eight—Uh-huh. She'll text you—What?! Are you kidding?—Fine, but don't you dare mess this up."

Marnyke leaned forward when Akira clicked off.

"I just got you a prom date who's gonna pretend to be Brodney," Akira said with a sigh. "And I only gotta pay him fifty bucks."

"He be late," Kiki declared. She looked stunning in her black gown. Her straight hair fell artfully over her right eye and her special sparkly makeup glinted in the bright lights of the San Marino lobby.

"He coming," Marnyke said stubbornly, holding her ground.

It was eight fifteen, and prom had already started. Kiki and Marnyke had arrived early to check out the Excelsior room. Big Boss had come through in a big way. The walls were decorated with floor-to-ceiling, blown-up yearbook photos, and each of the tables had a centerpiece of framed yearbook photos that the kids could take home plus a gorgeous display of spring flowers.

Now they were waiting for Devon.

"Brodney," Marnyke muttered to herself. "Call him Brodney."

She'd filled Kiki in on everything. Devon was a busboy at Citron and was studying to be an actor. Akira had caught Devon driving back to the city with his family. He'd be home by seven thirty. All afternoon, Marnyke had been texting him details about Brodney's life so that Devon could fake being Brodney.

"Well, when he get here, he gonna be with a deft girl," Kiki told Marnyke.

Marnyke forced a smile. Her prom dress was ultra-short, ultra-tight, and ultra-gold. It came off both shoulders and showed the tops of her breasts. Her makeup included gold eyeliner, and her gorgeous hair was held back by a spectacular gold headband. She'd turned a lot of heads when she came into the San Marino that was for sure.

"This be him." Marnyke showed Kiki a cell picture that Devon had uploaded. He looked a lot like the hip-hop artist K'naan, right down to the scraggly beard.

"Umm, Marnyke?" Kiki asked, poking Marnyke in the side. "I think he here."

Marnyke saw Kiki point to the left.

Yep. It was Devon.

"Gawd. He short!" Kiki exclaimed.

"And where he get that suit?" Marnyke moaned. Her jaw hung open. Devon wore a bright green suit with matching green shoes. He had on a black shirt and a green bow tie.

Devon spotted them. He trotted over, grinning wildly.

Marnyke stood. She wasn't more than five foot two but found herself looking down at her fake date.

"Hey, I'm Devon," the guy said, sticking out his hand.

"Marnyke," Marnyke managed. "This my bestie, Kiki."

"You look fly, girl," he said to Marnyke.

"Thanks. You look ..."

Marnyke searched for the right word. She didn't want to be mean. The guy was doing her a favor. Well, a fifty-buck favor, courtesy of her sister. "You look ... original!"

"I got my own style," Devon said proudly.

Marnyke tried to imagine walking into the prom with this tiny green guy on her arm.

She couldn't. But she had to.

She looped her arm gamely through Devon's.

"Okay," she declared. "Here we go."

CHAPTER
11

"Lemme hear you say hey, ho! Hey, ho! Hey, ho! Move yo' arms and say hey, ho! Hey, ho! Hey, ho!"

The city's most popular hip-hop star, Tone Def, pranced around the stage of the Excelsior Ballroom as everyone pressed close to the stage and swung their arms overhead. That Tone Def was performing was yet another stunner put together by Big Boss, who'd led everyone to think that some other band was entertaining.

Tone Def wore a bright orange tux and a matching top hat. His chest was bare under the jacket. As the students roared, he ripped off the jacket and flung it into the seething mass of kids. "Hey, ho! Hey, ho!"

The packed ballroom—every junior and senior had showed up—pulsed. Kiki moved off to find Sean; Marnyke and Devon got a little lost in the throng. That was fine, actually. The less contact Devon had with her YC friends, the better. She would do her best to make everyone believe that Devon was actually Brodney, but she didn't doubt that if Tia and Sherise had the chance to bust on her over a fake date, they would.

Some stuff just be too tempting.

She glanced to her right. By the far wall was the voting area for prom king and prom queen. She realized she hadn't made her choice, and that Darnell would surely be on the list for prom king. She was glad she hadn't seen him yet.

Devon was swinging his arms with everyone else as Tone Def launched into a tune about what would happen if Tim Tebow went ghetto. She poked him gently.

"I'm headin' over there!" She pointed to the voting area.

He gave her the okay sign, and she moved off through the crowd.

There was a senior girl in charge of the voting. She gave Marnyke a ballot and crossed Marnyke's name off a list. Marnyke checked out the ballot. For king, there was Darnell, of course, plus three other guys. One of them, D'Brickashaw Wenner, she knew a little. He was a huge guy: a really smart football lineman who'd always been decent to her. Marnyke remembered him saying in some class that he wanted to be a psychoanalyst—whatever that was!—after he was done with the NFL.

She stared at the ballot for a long minute. Then she marked a name and went on to prom queen. Here, too, there was really only one choice. Serene Jones. Everyone knew Serene. She was a senior and had something wrong with her legs. She was in a wheelchair more often than not.

I'm definitely votin' for Serene.

Tone Def finished his song; the crowd blew it up. Tone Def said he'd take a quick break—why didn't people hit up the buffet? The crowd in front of the stage scattered. Devon came over to Marnyke.

"You hungry?" he asked.

"Not much." She didn't want anything running down the front of her gown.

"Well, how 'bout we get some—"

"Marnyke! Wow! You lookin' fly!" Sherise came running over to them with Tia not far behind.

"Marnyke? Is this Brodney? You have to introduce us!" Tia demanded. "Right, Sherise?" Tia poked Sherise.

"Right!"

Damn. Sherise and Tia don't even like each other much. Why they gotta be all buddy-buddy now?

Marnyke saw the two girls share a not-so-secret smile.

I know what they thinkin'. This be *Brodney?*

She had no choice but to make the introduction.

"Sherise? Tia? Meet Brodney Wells. Brodney, this be Sherise and Tia. They in yearbook club with me."

"Hey, ladies," Devon said. He showed no nerves. "I'm Brodney. You looking very fine."

"Thanks," Tia answered as flirty as Tia Ramirez could be, which was not very flirty at all. "I hear you go to Spellman."

"That's right," Devon acknowledged with a smile. "Best black college in the country. I'm lucky they took me."

He really be an actor. Can he pull this off?

"That's a great school. Great town too. Atlanta. My mom's cousins live there. What's your favorite place to go out? How about your favorite restaurant? Who's your favorite professor?" Tia pressed.

She probin'. She totally probin' him.

"Excuse me?" Devon asked.

Marnyke tried to rescue her fake date. "What up with the questions, Tia? Let Brodney enjoy the prom."

"She just tryin' to get to know yo' date," Sherise jumped in. She then sidled closer to Devon. "You sure tall, Brodney."

Devon laughed. "That what Marnyke told you, right? We were messing with you. I may be short, but I'm mighty."

Tia laughed. "Oh, we're messed with all right. Aren't we, Sherise?"

"So messed," Sherise agreed.

Tia turned to Sherise. "Don't you ever get tired of hip-hop, Sherise?"

Sherise nodded. "Sometimes. Tone Def be butter, but sometimes a girl need a change."

"Yeah," Tia agreed. "I could use a change too. I'm sort of in the mood for something, I don't know, jazzy. Wow! Marnyke? Didn't you tell us Brodney played jazz piano?"

Marnyke nodded helplessly. She had said that when she'd first talked about Brodney in the cafeteria.

"There's this beautiful grand piano in the lobby!" Tia exclaimed. "Maybe Brodney can play for us!"

"Great idea!" Sherise agreed. "We can get everyone to come listen!"

Devon jumped in. He cleverly gripped his right wrist with his left hand. "I've got bad tendonitis. Can't play even if I wanted to. Not for two more months. Sorry."

He tryin'. He fightin' to help me. They know he ain't the real deal.

They gonna make me look real bad. They gonna tell everyone.

We gotta get out of here.

She took hold of Devon's arm.

"Come on, Brodney," she said. "Sherise, Tia, 'scuse us. We meetin' some people."

Without waiting for a response, Marnyke pulled Devon away. Together they headed for the doors. From behind her, Marnyke could hear Tia and Sherise's derisive laughter. Then they heard Tia's voice cut through the noise in the ballroom.

"I looked up Brodney's Facebook page! Marnyke! Your date isn't Brodney! You've got a fake date!"

"They nailed me." Devon pointed out the obvious.

Marnyke felt so upset she could barely see her way out the ballroom door. "You tried. Thanks."

"Where we goin'?"

Marnyke shook her head. She felt dead inside and tired. "Dunno. I gotta take a break."

"Me too," Devon told her.

"Meet me in twenty minutes, 'kay?"

"Where?" Devon asked.

Marnyke thought. "How 'bout right here? Then we can decide what to do."

Devon nodded. "It was a good try, Marnyke."

"I guess."

They went their separate ways. Marnyke ended up on a comfy couch in the busy lobby, not far from the grand piano. It was a good place. She didn't see anyone at all from school. She put down her handbag, closed her eyes, and tried to figure out what to do after she and Devon met up again. Could she really stand going back in the ballroom? Maybe the best thing to do was to call it a night and go—

"Hey. Bailing on your prom?"

She opened her eyes. Standing over her was a white boy she didn't know. He was about five foot nine and handsome in an off-kilter way—curly hair, scruffy stubble on his cheeks and chin, bushy eyebrows. He wore a black tux with a T-shirt under it. On the T-shirt was a printed tuxedo shirt and bowtie.

Okay. Thas funny.

"Bailing on your prom?" the guy repeated. "If you are, that makes two of us. I'm Gabe. May I join you?"

CHAPTER
12

Marnyke shrugged. She wasn't much into talking to white guys, but these were unusual circumstances. "Why not? They say misery love company."

"Thanks. I got enough for both of us."

Gabe sat with Marnyke's handbag between them. Marnyke saw Gabe's feet for the first time and grinned. He wore purple basketball shoes.

"Nice kicks," she quipped.

"Thanks. I wish my girlfriend thought so." He turned to her. Marnyke noticed he had smokin' green eyes. "I'm here to say that a person can get dumped at prom and live to tell the tale. Maybe."

Marnyke raised her eyebrows. "Your girlfriend waited till prom? My man did me a few days ago."

"But you're here," Gabe said. "You didn't get his memo?"

"I got it. It's a long story," she confessed glumly.

Gabe settled back. "My girlfriend's in there dancing with some other dude. So I'm kinda free for the evening."

Marnyke laughed. This boy was both funny and not afraid to make fun of himself. It was endearing. She was in no hurry to get back to her own prom. Who knew what fate awaited her back there.

She decided to introduce herself.

"I'm Marnyke Cooper. M-A-R-N-Y-K-E. Pronounced M-A-R-N-E-E-K. I go to South Central. How 'bout chu, Gabe?

You got a last name? I don't talk to just any ol' white boy, you know."

Gabe gave a little bow. "Samson. Gabe Samson. I go to Majestic Oaks."

"Majestic Oaks?" Majestic Oaks was the wealthiest suburb in the whole state. Few black folks lived there. Fewer than few. Marnyke whistled. "Damn. That's a rich town."

"My dad's kinda rich," Gabe admitted. "My mom's kinda rich too, but she doesn't live with my dad anymore." He smiled a lopsided smile, and Marnyke noticed he had a really cute dimple. He continued, "Me? My folks want me to go to college, but I just want to play with my band. That means I'm going to be a poor boy with a rich mom and dad."

"You're a senior then?"

Gabe nodded. "Got into a whole bunch of colleges. Not going to any of them."

"I'm a junior, an' I don't know if I'm ever goin' to college," Marnyke told him.

"That makes two of us again," Gabe replied. "You know about my night. Why don't you tell me about yours?"

"Why should I?"

Gabe looked a little sheepish. "I'm in no hurry to get back to my prom. And I'm a good listener."

Maybe it was because she knew she'd never see Gabe again. Maybe it was to put off going back to the prom for as long as she could. Maybe it was those eyes. Maybe it was all three. Whatever the reason, Marnyke told him the whole story of Darnell, Brodney, and Devon. She even mentioned her mother in prison.

"I've got a relative in prison too," he said easily.

"Your mom?" Marnyke was both shocked and secretly thrilled. It was a strange but powerful connection.

Gabe shook his head. "An uncle. For fraud. I never liked him much anyway."

Marnyke's phone buzzed with a text. She checked it. Devon.

> U comin?

She puffed out some air audibly. "My fake date."

"You going back?"

"I guess I should," she said and started to rearrange herself.

"Well, you're definitely the most beautiful girl in the hotel. That guy Darnell is a flipping idiot. Hold your head high. You've got nothing to be ashamed of."

Marnyke smiled. She liked this guy.

Too bad I'll never see him again.

Gabe took out his cell—a crappy feature phone like Marnyke's. Marnyke was surprised. Gabe noticed.

"My dad offered me an Android, but I only want what I can afford," he explained.

"I like that."

"I like you. I wonder if I could get your digits. Maybe we can stay in touch," he suggested. "You saved my night."

"No. You saved mine."

Marnyke, as a rule, did not give her phone number to guys she met in the lobbies of gorgeous hotels. Especially white guys who went to Majestic Oaks High School.

Some rules were made to be broken.

She shared her number. He gave her his. Then they both stood.

"Text me anytime," he told her. "It's going to be a weird rest of the evening."

"That's for damn sure," she agreed.

He held out his hand. She shook it. Then he gave a little wave and was on his way back to his prom. She watched him cut through the lobby in his tux with the purple basketball shoes. Somehow, for this guy, it worked.

On her way back to the Excelsior Ballroom, Marnyke made up her mind what she wanted to do. She was going to meet Devon, and they were going to dance. If Tia and Sherise gave her a hard time, she'd tell them to go to hell.

She expected to find Devon outside. He wasn't there, though. Tone Def was in the middle of another number, and the music pounded through the doors. She was about to go inside and look for him when she heard Kiki call her name.

"Marnyke?"

She turned. There was Kiki with Sean. He wore a garish white tux. Behind her were Sherise and Carlos, Tia and Ty, and Nishell and Jackson. There'd clearly been some advance planning since the guys were in tuxes that matched Sean's.

Well, well. It's a full-court press.

"Hi," she said to Kiki. "Where's Devon?"

One more surprise. Sherise answered her instead of Kiki. "Devon's inside. We introduced him to Serene. I think they like each other."

"Devon's cool," Tia added.

Whoa. What's goin' on? What did I miss?

"I talked to everyone," Kiki confessed. "Actually, Devon and I talked to everyone. Before I introduced him to Serene. I figured that was okay with you."

"Fine with me," Marnyke told them.

"He's moonin' all over her. Good thing she didn't have a date," Nishell joked.

Tia stepped forward. "Sherise and I blew it. I know you don't like me, and I know you don't like her much, either. But I've never felt beautiful in my whole life. Not till tonight, thanks to you. Devon told us all about what happened with Brodney. I had no right to get up in your you-know-what."

Sherise took a step forward too. "What she said."

Marnyke had a decision to make. She could accept their apology or tell them that they were mean, evil, nasty—

Let it go. Better story if I let it go. Besides, I got something big to do.

"We good," she told Tia and Sherise. "We aight. Did they crown the prom king yet?"

Sherise shook head. "Soon, I think."

"I don't want to miss that. Let's go in."

They went inside and stood together. The timing was perfect. Mr. Crandall—Marnyke thought she'd never seen anyone look sillier in a tux—was on stage with a microphone. He stood next to Tone Def. They were the oddest pair in history, but they were ready to do the honors.

Crandall cleared his throat.

"Yo, Crandall!" Someone shouted from the back. "Nice pic in the yearbook!"

A wave of laughter and hooting rolled through the ballroom.

Marnyke thought Crandall would be pissed at this reference to the photograph of his bare rear end that had been hacked into the yearbook.

Instead, the guidance counselor managed a smile. "I like to show my better side," he cracked.

There was a moment of stunned silence.

Had Crandall actually made a joke?

There were a few uneasy laughs. Then more. Then people roared with laughter, whooped, and cheered as Crandall gave the mic and a folded sheet of paper to Tone Def. Behind them on stage were the four nominees for prom king and the four for prom queen.

"So, y'all, first I wan' you to give it up for Big Boss. He didn' come tonight because he wanted this party to be 'bout you 'stead of 'bout him, but let's show some props. Give it up for Big Boss!"

The place went absolutely nuts. Marnyke cheered and clapped as loud as anyone.

"Now it be time to announce your prom king and queen," Tone Def roared. "Here be your new queen."

He opened the sheet of paper and read a name. "Serene Jones!"

The crowd roared with joy as Serene rolled forward in her wheelchair pushed by the happy Devon. She wore a white sequined gown with a white scarf, and Marnyke thought she'd never looked cuter. Tone Def grinned as he put the crown on her head.

"And now for your king!" The audience hushed. Tone Def milked the moment. "This year's South Central High School prom king is ..."

Marnyke locked eyes with Darnell for two full seconds.

I hope you—

"D'Brickashaw Wenner!"

Again, the crowd erupted in cheers as D'Brickashaw bounded forward to accept the crown. Tone Def was tall, but he had to reach way up to get the crown on the huge football player's head. When the crown was safely on, D'Brickashaw popped some moves with surprising grace for someone so big. The crowd loved it.

Meanwhile, Darnell just looked crushed.

"Join the prom king and queen in a dance, y'all," Tone Def shouted.

The music turned slow and romantic. There was one more roar of approval as powerful D'Brickashaw got an okay from

Devon then scooped up petite Serene in his arms and stepped down to the dance floor.

Everyone hit the floor. Kiki and Sean. Jackson and Nishell. Ty and Tia. Sherise and Carlos. Even Devon and Misha. They were swaying to the music, clinging to each other, happy as could be. After a few moments, D'Brickashaw graciously beckoned for Devon to come dance with Serene. Devon rolled the wheelchair off the stage; D'Brickashaw set Serene in it. Then Devon took Serene's hands and danced with her.

Marnyke stood alone, taking it all in.

Darnell stood across the dance floor. Alone.

Marnyke made a decision. She crossed the floor and offered him her hand. "Dance, Darnell?"

He nodded. They found an open space, and she moved into his arms. She kept her distance. She wasn't going to let him draw her in, but they were dancing just the same.

"Thanks, Mar," Darnell murmured. "You look finger lickin' good."

"Shut it down, Darnell. You shoulda been my date tonight," she said bluntly.

"I know," he admitted.

"I voted for you anyway," she said.

He stopped dancing and stepped away from her. "You what?"

"I voted for you, for prom king," she repeated. "You a big basketball star. You goin' away to college. You got outta the life. You gonna make something of your life. You got my vote, Darnell, tonight. Win or lose."

Marnyke couldn't be certain, but she thought she saw a tear in her ex-boyfriend's eye. Then she felt tears form in her own.

"Let's leave it at that," she added softly. "Okay?"

He nodded. "Okay. Good luck, Marnyke."

"Luck to you, Darnell."

Marnyke eased herself between the dancing couples and off the dance floor. As she did, Crandall stopped her.

"Marnyke?"

"Yes, Mr. Crandall?"

He seemed to compose himself, looking for just the right words. "I just wanted to say, good job on your essay. I didn't know you had it in you."

Marnyke nodded. "Thank you. Neither did I."

She moved off to stand alone again, gazing out at her friends and frenemies. Everyone seemed so pumped and happy. That was good. She was solo, though. That was bad.

"Don't need to be," she told herself.

She took out her phone and scrolled through her contacts to a new one. Then she punched in a quick text to Gabe.

> Wanna dance?

It felt like she'd barely pressed Send before a text came back to her.

> Yr prom or mine?

That was the answer she wanted.

> Mine. We got Tone Def

Again, she barely had to wait for his return text.

> C U in 5

Perfect.